Five reasons why you'll

love Mirabelle . . .

Mirabelle is magical
and mischievous!

Mirabelle is half
witch, half fairy, and
totally naughty!

She loves making
potions with her travelling
potion kit!

Mirabelle loves sprinkling
a sparkle of mischief
wherever she goes!

She has a
little baby dragon
called Violet!

If you went on holiday with a witch what would you do for fun?

Make sandcastle mermaids and make a magic potion to turn them alive!
– Betsy, age 4

Make lots of ice cream and the biggest sandcastle, but then cause mischief and swap everyone's ice cream flavours for broccoli flavour.
– Mia, age 6

Make a potion to make a fun waterslide and become a merwitch and go swimming with dolphins, topped off with a witch feast. Yummy.
– Lyra, age 6

Make a dragon to take us to the moon!
– Tabitha, age 6

Make dragons appear, make people tiny, and cast spells.
– Grace, age 6

Go on a witch carousel with lots of broomsticks and then we would fly to the beach and make giant sandcastles.
– Matilda, age 7

I would go broomstick waterskiing!
– Sophia, age 5

Family Tree

My Mum
Seraphina Starspell

My brother
Wilbur Starspell

My Dad
Alvin Starspell

Me!
Mirabelle Starspell

Violet

Illustrated by Mike Love, based on
original artwork by Harriet Muncaster

Great Clarendon Street, Oxford OX2 6DP

Oxford University Press is a department of the University of Oxford.
It furthers the University's objective of excellence in research, scholarship, and
education by publishing worldwide. Oxford is a registered trade mark of Oxford
University Press in the UK and in certain other countries

British Library Cataloguing in Publication Data

Data available

ISBN: 978-0-19-277756-0

1 3 5 7 9 10 8 6 4 2

Printed in China

Paper used in the production of this book is a natural,
recyclable product made from wood grown in sustainable forests.
The manufacturing process conforms to the environmental
regulations of the country of origin.

From the world of  ISADORA MOON

MIRABELLE

in Double Trouble

Harriet Muncaster

OXFORD
UNIVERSITY PRESS

Chapter ONE

'Did you pack your fairy wand, Mirabelle?' asked Dad as we all stood by the front door with our suitcases, waiting for Mum.

'Er . . . I think I forgot,' I said.

Dad sighed. He's a fairy and is always trying to get me to use my wand more often, but the truth is that I prefer to use witch magic like Mum! I just *feel* more

witch most of the time even though I am *technically* half fairy too, along with my brother, Wilbur.

'There's still time to go and fetch it,' said Dad, glancing at his watch. 'And while you're at it you can tell Mum to hurry up. We don't want to be late for check in! She's probably packing all her lotions and potions.'

My mum and dad own their own beauty business concocting organic face creams, perfumes, and lipsticks. Mum can spend all day up in her witch turret experimenting with ingredients and sometimes it's hard to tear her away from work!

'OK,' I said.

I ran off up the stairs with my pet dragon, Violet, flapping along behind me. I felt a fizzle of excitement in my tummy. We were packing for holiday—to stay in a treehouse at an all-inclusive witch resort in the mountains. There was going to be a bubbling cauldron hot tub and a waterpark with a twirly witch's hat slide! I couldn't wait!

'Mum!' I called as I ran past her bedroom. 'Dad says you need to hurry!'

'I'll be there in just a moment,' Mum called.

I skidded into my bedroom and looked around for my fairy wand. Maybe it would be useful to bring it after all? I could use it to magic up some fairy food to eat while we were away. Fairy food is way nicer than witch food.

Eventually I found my wand and pulled it out from the bottom of my toy chest. As I did so, I stared wistfully at my

witch's travelling potion kit which was
arranged proudly on my bedside table. I
had promised Mum and Dad I would leave
it at home.

'It always gets you into mischief,
Mirabelle!' Mum had said. 'Dad and I
would like a break this holiday. You can
bring your fairy wand but no witch magic.
It's too unpredictable.'

So I had promised to leave my witch's travelling potion kit at home.

And I had promised to be really good all holiday.

And I really did mean it.

I looked at my fairy wand and then I looked at my witch's travelling potion kit. What harm could it do to just have both of them with me? Mum and Dad didn't need to know. I stuffed my witch kit under my jumper and ran downstairs waving my fairy wand.

'Got it!' I said to Dad and quickly bent down, making a great show of unzipping my suitcase to put it inside, but also slipping my witch kit in too.

'Right!' said Dad, rubbing his hands. 'Here's Mum too, at last. Let's go. I can't wait to get to that lovely forest and absorb all the beautiful nature!'

The drive to the mountain forest seemed to go on forever. Dad is *such* a nervous driver he goes really slowly to the point that cars line up behind us, hooting and tooting.

'You should have let me drive!' grumbled Mum, as she sat in the passenger seat and applied a layer of dark purple lipstick. 'We would have arrived by now!'

'Absolutely not,' said Dad. 'You drive like a daredevil!'

Mum huffed but I secretly felt glad that Dad was driving us rather than Mum, even if we were travelling at a snail's pace. Mum can be quite . . . *frightening* behind the wheel.

The truth is that neither of my parents are very good at driving. They don't get a lot of practice because if they need to go somewhere they usually fly. Dad has fairy wings and Mum has a broomstick.

At last we were driving through countryside along some narrow winding roads. The landscape had become quite hilly and I could see mountains in the distance.

'Ah!' said Dad. 'Isn't nature magnificent!'

'Are we nearly there?' I asked.

'Nearly,' said Mum.

Wilbur didn't say anything. He was

totally absorbed in his book of Wizard's

Wordsearches. I pressed my nose against

the window as we approached the mountains. Soon we were driving along roads lined with tall fir trees and the atmosphere became a little dark and creepy. Dad put his headlights on even though it was only late afternoon.

'Ooh!' said Mum, rubbing her hands together with glee. 'This feels *witchy!*'

'It does doesn't it,' said Dad a little nervously. 'Ah, well here we are!' He turned off the road and pulled into a car park. We all jumped out of the car. Right ahead of us was a huge wooden building with pointy roofs shaped like witches' hats.

'The Great Hall!' said Mum. 'This is where the main office and the restaurant are. I'll just go and check in and then we can go and find our treehouse!'

Mum disappeared into the Great Hall while Wilbur, Dad, and I waited in the car park. In the distance we could hear

the faint sound of cackling, and a thin trail of smoke wound up into the sky from somewhere nearby. Dad shivered.

'It is a bit spookier here than I thought it would be,' he said. 'Where are the flowers, and the baby animals skipping about? The trees look rather dark and spindly to me.'

'It's a *witch* resort,' I reminded him.

'Just focus on the nature, Dad,' said Wilbur, patting him on the shoulder.

It wasn't long before Mum reappeared, jangling a set of keys.

'We have to follow the forest path,' she said. 'And it's the sixth tree on the left! Come on everyone!'

She opened the car boot and began to heave our suitcases out while Dad closed his eyes and breathed deeply.

'*All* nature is beautiful,' he kept whispering under his breath. '*All* nature is beautiful.'

'What *are* you doing, Alvin?' said Mum, slamming the boot of the car shut again.

'Oh . . . er . . . nothing!' said Dad, quickly opening his eyes and holding his hand out for his suitcase.

Chapter TWO

As we walked along the path, I gazed
upwards marvelling at the beautiful
treehouses that had been built high up
in the branches. They were all different
shapes and sizes and they all had roofs
shaped like pointed witches' hats. I
could see witches and wizards sitting in
deckchairs up high on wooden platforms,

sipping fancy drinks and cackling.

'Here we are!' said Mum as we reached a large family-sized treehouse with a spiral of wooden steps running all the way up the trunk. 'Home for the week!'

'Yay!' I shouted, and raced all the way up the steps to the top, getting there before Wilbur. Our treehouse was amazing! There was a big open sitting room with a round black stove in the middle of it, two bedrooms and a small kitchen and bathroom. Outside on the deck was the big cauldron-shaped hot tub.

'Looks like we'll be sharing a room, Wilby!' I shouted gleefully.

Wilbur didn't look pleased.

'Aww Mum, you said I could have my own room!' he said.

'Oh, did I?' said Mum. 'Sorry Wilbur, it looks as though there are only two bedrooms so you will have to share.'

Wilbur looked disgruntled and I found myself feeling surprisingly hurt. I know we sometimes get on each other's nerves but I had been quite looking forward to sharing a room with my big brother for a week.

'Oh, come on Wilbur,' I said. 'It will be fun! We can talk late into the night and sneak into the kitchen for a midnight feast!'

'I heard that!' came Mum's voice from the other room.

We spent the next hour unpacking and settling in to our treehouse.

'I'm getting straight into the hot tub!' I declared, changing into my swimming costume as fast as I could. I ran out onto the balcony and jumped into the giant cauldron with a splash! It was much warmer than I had been expecting.

'Ooh!' I panted. I could feel my cheeks
turning red as the water bubbled all
around me and the steam rose off it in lilac
clouds.

'Slowly and gently does it,' said Dad,
sticking his toe in gingerly. 'You have to
ease yourself in Mirabelle. *Ease* yourself
in.'

By the time Dad had finally got into
the water Mum and Wilbur were already

fully in and my body
had got used to the
temperature. Mum had
brought out a platter of
jellied insects and she
was popping them into
her mouth like sweets.

'Ahhh!' she said, as beetle juice
dripped down her chin. 'This is the life!'

I wrinkled my nose at Wilbur and he
wrinkled his back at me.

'Yuck!' we both said.

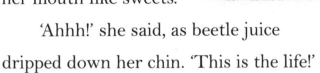

Once we had all had a nice long go in the
hot tub Mum suggested that we go back

29

to the Great Hall.

'We can book some activities while we're there,' she said. 'And then we can have dinner afterwards! There's a lovely restaurant that serves all kinds of witch delicacies.'

'I think I'll bring a lunchbox,' said Dad quickly. 'I packed some honey sandwiches for just such an occasion.'

'Can I have honey sandwiches too, Dad?' I asked.

'And me,' said Wilbur.

There were lots of other witch and wizard families milling about the Great Hall. I ran up to a big board with lots of posters showing all the different activities we could do.

'I want to go to the waterpark!' I said, pointing.

'I want to go swamp swimming,' said Wilbur.

'I want to go dragon trekking!' said another voice next to us.

I turned to see a girl, a little bit shorter than me,

31

standing in front of the board with her mum and dad. She had spirally curls and a cheeky expression on her face.

'I don't know, Beatrix,' her dad was saying. 'Last time we went dragon trekking you got up to all kinds of mischief.'

'Yes,' sighed her mum. 'We were hoping for a *break* from mischief this holiday.'

I glanced at Beatrix and smiled.

Beatrix smiled back at me.

A flicker of mischief passed between us.

'Hello! I'm Mirabelle Starspell,' I said holding out my hand for her to shake.

'Beatrix Hemlock,' she replied.

Wilbur stared at us both and took a
step back.

'Uh oh,' he said.

Chapter THREE

It wasn't long before Mum and Dad
were deep in conversation with Beatrix's
parents and we all decided to go to the
restaurant together. Beatrix and I sat next
to each other and exchanged stories about
all the tricks we had played.

'I once turned my Dad into a frog by
mistake!' I giggled.

'Oh really!?' said Beatrix, but she
didn't look quite as impressed as I thought
she would be.

'I once turned my teacher into a
lizard!'

I gasped.

'Your *teacher*?'

'Yes,' whispered Beatrix. 'I got into a lot of trouble.'

'Oh,' I said. Then I remembered something.

'I once made *my* teacher's hair grow really, really long,' I said. 'She was furious!'

'I bet!' said Beatrix. 'That reminds *me* of the time that I made everyone in my classroom go bald. For *five whole days!*'

I stared at Beatrix, gobsmacked, and she nodded, looking pleased with herself. I had never met anyone as naughty as Beatrix before.

We could have a *lot* of fun together.

But we could also get into a *lot* of trouble together.

And I had promised Mum and Dad
that there would be absolutely no mischief
this holiday.

After dinner we waved goodbye to
Beatrix's family and went back to our
treehouse. We had all decided to go
dragon trekking the next day.

'I can't wait!' said Wilbur as he
snuggled down into bed. 'I've always
wanted to go dragon trekking.'

'Me too!' I said, getting into my
own bed and pulling Violet close to my
chest for a hug. I wondered if I ought to
suggest a midnight feast to Wilbur but

I was already feeling quite full from the honey sandwiches and quite sleepy. It had been a tiring and interesting day. 'Maybe tomorrow night,' I thought, as I drifted off into sleep.

Chapter
FOUR

The following day I woke up to sunshine
streaming through the treehouse window
and the sound of leaves rustling outside.

'Sunshine!' cried Dad happily as he
burst into mine and Wilbur's room. 'How
cheering! Time to get up, you two. We're
meeting Beatrix's family to go dragon
trekking, remember?'

'Oh yes!' I said, jumping out of bed and feeling a tingle of excitement in my toes. I hurriedly got dressed, and then went out onto the deck where Mum was having her usual breakfast of spider sprinkled toast and Dad had used his wand to magic up some flower petal fairy yoghurt.

'You ought to practise using your fairy wand, Mirabelle,' said Dad. 'I'd like

to see you magic up your own breakfast with it this morning.'

I hurried off to my room and rummaged in my suitcase to find my wand. It was right at the bottom sitting alongside my witch kit.

'What's that?' asked Wilbur, coming to peer over my shoulder.

'What's what?' I asked, closing the lid of my suitcase quickly. I felt my cheeks turn a bit pink.

'I saw some of your witch things in there!' said Wilbur. 'I thought Mum and Dad told you not to bring them.'

'Oh, well . . . ' I began. 'I . . . '

'Mirabelle!' said Wilbur. 'You'd better

not be planning to play any tricks on me!'

'I'm not planning anything!' I said.
'I'm not going to use it. I bet *you* brought
your wizards things.'

'I'm *allowed* to bring my wizard
things,' said Wilbur, 'because I'm sensible
with them!'

He looked so smug that I felt
immediately cross.

'Just don't tell Mum and Dad,' I
huffed, and stomped out of the room with

my fairy wand.

I cheered up when Mum and Dad
let me magic up whatever I wanted as a
special holiday treat. I had chocolate cake
for breakfast with a strawberry crush
drink.

'Very good, Mirabelle!' said Dad
approvingly as I waved my wand above
my plate, sending stars and sparkles
flurrying through the air. 'You see, fairy
magic isn't all boring!'

'No,' I agreed as I munched on my
cake.

After breakfast we walked back to the
Great Hall where we met Beatrix's family
for the dragon trekking.

'Hello, Mirabelle!' shouted Beatrix
happily. She was wearing a full explorer's
outfit and had a pair of binoculars hanging
round her neck.

'Hi, Beatrix!' I smiled. We didn't have
much time to talk because
the tour guide suddenly
appeared and beckoned for
us all to follow him into the
forest. We walked down a
winding path away from
the treehouses until we got

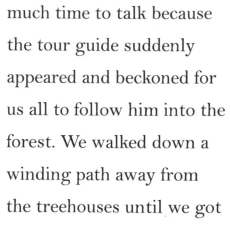

44

to an enclosure where there were lots of dragons happily snoozing and crunching on charcoal. They were big!

'They're almost the size of the dragon I once magicked up with my cousin Isadora!' I whispered to Beatrix. 'She took it to school. We got in a whole load of trouble.'

'Really!' said Beatrix. 'That reminds me of the time that I magicked up a dragon and let it loose in the supermarket!'

I stared at her.

'Did you *really* do that?' I asked.

'Yes,' said Beatrix. 'Ooh look at that green dragon there! I'm going to ask the tour guide if I can ride that one!'

'I want to ride the purple one,' I said. 'With the shimmery scales.'

The tour guide showed us all how to put a saddle and reigns onto our chosen dragons and then we were allowed to climb up and sit on top of them.

'Look at me!' cried Wilbur as he proudly sat on top of a huge blue spotty dragon. He twitched the reign and his dragon began to plod forwards on its claws.

'Well done, everyone!' said the tour guide from the front of the group. 'Now remember, we are not going to fly the dragons. It's against health and safety regulations. We are just going to let them walk in a line through the forest and look at the scenery. That's why it's called dragon *trekking*.'

'But what if the dragon wants to fly?' asked someone in the group. 'What do we do then?'

'You don't need to worry,' said the tour guide. 'The dragons have all been trained to stay on the ground as long as they have a rider on their back. Right, is everyone ready? Let's go!'

The dragons all started walking towards a little path between the trees. It was lovely sitting on the dragon's back and being gently bounced up and down as we made our way through the sunshiny leaves. Violet fluttered by my shoulder. I think she felt a bit confused to see so many large dragons all in one place! Every now and then we stopped while the tour guide pointed at something for us to look at and I saw Beatrix peer through her binoculars. After a while she sidled up to me on her dragon so that we were walking side by side.

'Don't you think it would be fun
if our dragons went a little faster?' she
whispered.

'Yes,' I agreed, because it was true. It
would be more fun to go a little faster.

Beatrix whipped out a potion bottle
from one of her many explorer's pockets
and pulled out the stopper.

'I've brought something we can use
to make our dragons go faster!' she said.

'I'm going to use it on mine. Do you
want me to splash some of the
potion on yours?'

'Oh, er . . .' I said,
remembering my promise
to Mum and Dad about not

causing any mischief. But then, did this *really* count as mischief? We were just going to make our dragons go a little bit faster, that was all. I didn't see what harm it would do. All the tour guide had said was no *flying*.

'OK!' I said. 'I'll have some of the potion!'

Beatrix came a bit closer and when no one was looking she splashed a bit of the potion on my dragon's back before doing the same to her dragon.

The effect was immediate.

My dragon sped right up! It began cantering forwards, overtaking Wilbur and Dad and all the dragons in the line.

I gripped onto the reigns and hunched down, a little afraid that I might fall off but mostly just really excited. This was so much fun!

'Woo hoo!' yelled Beatrix, and I turned my head to see her hurtling down

the forest path behind me. She had a big grin on her face and her hair was flying out behind her.

'Mirabelle?' shouted Mum as I whipped past her. 'Slow down!'

Oops.

Maybe we *were* going a little fast.

I pulled on my dragon's reins and it slowed down a little bit, just as Beatrix came whooshing past, shrieking in delight.

'Has your potion stopped working?' she asked as she zipped ahead.

'No . . .' I began to explain.

'Here have some more!' said Beatrix. She flung her arm back and I saw a stream of potion arc through the air before landing on my dragon's head.

My dragon began to speed up again and this time no amount of pulling on the reigns would slow him down.

'Stop right now!' shouted the tour guide from quite far behind. 'Everyone must stay behind me!'

But my dragon just kept bounding forward, faster and faster. It was going even faster than Beatrix's dragon now! It was going so fast that it was starting to flap its wings and fly up into the air. It started to do loop the loops. I held onto its neck for dear life.

'Heeeelp!' I shrieked.

I could see the row of dragon

trekkers down below.
Everyone, including Beatrix,
had now stopped and was
staring up at me in horror.

'Mirabelle!' shrieked
Mum from far away, her eyes

wide and panicked. 'Don't let go! I haven't got my broomstick!'

But my hands were already beginning to slip away from around my dragon's neck.

I screwed my eyes shut tightly.

And started to fall.

Down . . .

Down . . .

Down . . .

Until suddenly I felt myself land heavily in someone's arms.

Someone who said 'OOF!'

And I opened my eyes to see Dad hovering in the air looking both cross and relieved at the same time.

'Thank goodness for fairy wings!' he said.

'MIRABELLE STARSPELL!' said Mum when I landed back down on the ground with Dad. She hopped off her dragon and stormed over to me. I stepped backwards. Mum can be quite scary when she gets angry.

'Wait!' I said. 'I can explain!'

'*I* can explain,' said Wilbur. 'I think Mirabelle used a potion to make her dragon go faster. She's brought her potion kit on this holiday!'

'Wilbur!' I gasped.

'Is that true?' asked Mum. Her eyes had gone all dark and glinty like

blackberries. Dad just looked disappointed. I nodded my head sorrowfully.

'I haven't used it though,' I began. 'I didn't

make the potion. I can explain!'

But Mum didn't let me explain. She took me by the arm and dragged me back through the forest all the way to our treehouse with Wilbur and Dad following behind.

'Can't we finish the dragon trekking?' I heard Wilbur asking.

'No we can't!' fumed Mum. 'We're going back to the treehouse until it's time for dinner.'

'But that's so unfair!' whined Wilbur. 'It's not my fault Mirabelle used a potion!"

'I *didn't* use a potion!' I cried.

But no one listened.

Back at the treehouse Wilbur was in a very bad mood. He put his headphones on and sat on his bed, absorbed in his book of Wizards Wordsearches. I lay back on mine, stroking Violet and staring at the ceiling. I knew why Mum and Dad thought that the dragon trekking incident was all my fault. It was because usually things *were* my fault. And Wilbur spotting my (now confiscated) potion kit hadn't helped at all.

Chapter FIVE

That evening when we arrived in the
Great Hall for dinner we spotted Beatrix
and her family and we sat with them.

'Mirabelle!' said Beatrix, smiling.

'Hi, Beatrix,' I said unenthusiastically.
I couldn't help feeling rather annoyed with
her.

'Mirabelle!' she said again, in a more

whispery voice this time. 'I am SO sorry! I really didn't mean to get you into trouble like that! I thought your potion wasn't working and I was just trying to help you!'

'Really?' I said.

'Of course,' said Beatrix. 'I didn't hear the guide telling us to slow down until it was too late. Please forgive me. I'm really, really sorry!'

'OK,' I smiled. 'I forgive you.'

Beatrix smiled back. 'Thank you,' she said.

'And just so you know, my parents are cross with me too. They saw me whizz ahead with you on my dragon.'

'My Mum and Dad have calmed down now,' I said, 'but Wilbur is still really annoyed. He's not speaking to me *and* he told tales on me!'

'He told tales on you!' gasped Beatrix.

'Yes,' I said, explaining about my witch kit.

'But that's so unfair!' said Beatrix.

'I know,' I said. 'But you know what big brothers are like. I'm sure he'll get over it soon.'

'Hmm,' said Beatrix. Then she slid off her chair. 'I just need the toilet,' she said. 'I'll be back in a minute. If the waiter comes, tell my parents to order the beetle burger for me.'

'OK,' I said.

By the time Beatrix came back all the food had arrived and Dad had magicked up vegetarian mushroom spaghetti for himself, Wilbur, and me. We all started to tuck in.

'Mmm!' said Beatrix next to me as she munched on her beetle burger. 'Delicious.'

'Mine's yummy too!' I said, twirling the spaghetti round my fork.

Suddenly, I saw something flick across the table and over my plate, towards Wilbur's plate.

'What was that?' I asked.

'I didn't see anything!' said Beatrix and her eyes were very big and round.

'ARGHHHH!' screamed Wilbur, leaping out of his chair and pointing at his plate.

'WORMS!!!' he shouted.

I stared in horror at Wilbur's spaghetti which had turned into a squirming pile of worms. I leapt off my own chair feeling a bit sick.

'MIRABELLE!' shouted Wilbur.

'It wasn't me!' I gasped. 'I didn't do it! How could I? My potion kit's been

confiscated!'

'You must have!' said Wilbur. 'You were just getting me back for telling Mum and Dad about your potion kit!'

'I *wasn't!*' I insisted.

I glared at Beatrix but she didn't say anything. She just kept eating her burger.

'You were!' shouted Wilbur. He grabbed a fistful of worms and threw them at me.

'ARGHGHGH!' I screamed as the worms landed all over my hair, slimy and squirmy and disgusting. I grabbed

a handful of my spaghetti and threw it at Wilbur. It landed all over his wizard's hat making the silver stars all greasy.

'Food fight!' said Beatrix, looking up, her eyes glittering with delight.

Wilbur looked so cross that I thought he might explode. He grabbed his water glass and sloshed it all over me.

'WILBUR!' shouted Mum.

I grabbed my water glass and sloshed it all over Wilbur.

'MIRABELLE!' yelled Dad.

Wilbur picked up his bread roll and lobbed it into my face.

68

'BOTH OF YOU STOP IT THIS INSTANT!' shouted Mum. Her eyes were blazing. Like two tiny angry currants.

'WE ARE GOING BACK TO THE TREEHOUSE!' she said. 'I don't know what's got into you both!' and she marched us right out of the restaurant with Dad bobbing along behind, carrying his plate of mushroom spaghetti.

'No point in wasting it,' he said.

That night Wilbur and I were in disgrace.

'You can both go to your bedroom and stay there!' said Mum. 'GOODNIGHT!'

I sat down heavily on my bed and clutched Violet to my chest. I hadn't turned Wilbur's spaghetti into worms. Of course I hadn't! It was all Beatrix!

I felt very, very cross. And quite hungry.

Wilbur was cross too. He stomped over to his bed and picked up his headphones.

'Wilbur I swear I didn't turn your spaghetti into worms. It was Beatrix!'

Wilbur turned round. He narrowed his eyes disbelievingly.

'Really?'

'Yes!' I said. 'She disappeared off to the toilet for ages. I think she was making

70

a potion pellet. Then during dinner I think she flicked it onto your plate. Please believe me Wilbur!'

'I don't know,' said Wilbur, but he looked slightly less angry.

'And this morning too!' I continued. 'Everything that happened at the dragon trekking. That was Beatrix too! I know I packed my potion kit but I never even used it.'

'Hmm,' said Wilbur. 'If you're telling the truth, that means Beatrix is even naughtier than you!'

I felt my cheeks turn red. I don't mean to be naughty. Trouble just seems to follow me around.

'You need to tell Beatrix that you don't want any more tricks or mischief!' said Wilbur.

'I guess,' I said. Right at the moment I didn't feel like I ever wanted to see Beatrix again.

'Tell her tomorrow, Mirabelle. We're both in trouble because of her and I don't want any more tricks played on *me!*'

'OK,' I said. 'I will. I'm sorry she played a trick on you. Let me make it up to you, Wilbur. I'll magic up something really nice for you to eat with my fairy wand. What do you want?'

Wilbur perked up. He hadn't brought his wand on the holiday. He's rather

embarrassed about his fairy heritage.

'Spaghetti?' I suggested.

Wilbur turned a little green.

'I don't think I can ever eat spaghetti again,' he groaned. 'I know! Let's start with pudding. I'd like a big ice cream sundae with whipped cream on top and chocolate flakes and sliced bananas.'

'Coming right up!' I said and waved my wand. *Swish!* A flurry of sparks twinkled round the room and a delicious-looking chocolate and banana sundae

appeared on Wilbur's bedside table.
Wilbur picked it up and peered at it
suspiciously for a moment. Then he began
to dig in. I waved my wand again and
magicked up something similar for myself,
but this time with raspberries and toffee
sauce on top.

Twenty minutes later Wilbur lay back down on his bed rubbing his tummy.

'I'm so full!' he said. 'But that was fun, Mirabelle.'

He grinned at me and I grinned back, before waving my wand to get rid of any of the evidence.

'Sometimes hanging out with you isn't all *that* bad,' said Wilbur.

'Watch it, Wilbur!' I said, throwing my pillow at him.

'Ugh,' said Wilbur. 'I'm too full for a pillow fight! We'll have one tomorrow night.'

Chapter SIX

The following morning Wilbur and I
came sheepishly out of our bedroom and
slunk towards the breakfast table.

'Good morning!' said Dad cheerfully
as he basked in the sunshine.

'I hope it *will* be a good morning,'
said Mum who was wearing a large pair
of witchy sunglasses and her black silk

dressing gown.

'Let's try and have absolutely no mischief today shall we?'

'I promise!' I said.

'Good,' smiled Mum. 'All is forgiven then. Let's start afresh. I thought we could go to the waterpark today!'

'Oh yeah!' said Wilbur, punching the air with his fist.

We arrived at the waterpark and I gazed in wonderment at all the rides. There were some witchy bubbling rapids, a tube slide shaped like a snake with a fanged mouth to woosh out from, and loads of inflatable black cats that you could ride on.

'Woah!' said Wilbur, staring up at the giant black witch's hat slide. 'It's so high!'

'Let's go on it first!' I said.

We left our towels with Mum and
Dad and we were just about to climb the
steps when I heard a familiar voice behind
me.

'Mirabelle!'

'Uh oh,' said Wilbur.

My heart sank as I
turned around to see Beatrix
in a black bat swimming
costume.

'Mirabelle, I'm so sorry
about yesterday!' she said. '
I didn't mean to get you into
trouble.' She eyed Wilbur and
then whispered in my ear:
'I thought you'd be pleased!

79

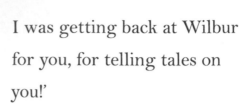

I was getting back at Wilbur for you, for telling tales on you!'

I frowned.

'I didn't need you to do that for me, Beatrix,' I said firmly.

'I know that now,' said Beatrix. 'It all got out of hand. And I really am sorry! Do you forgive me?'

I looked at Beatrix, kind of wishing that I could just spend some time with Wilbur at the pool. It would be much safer! But I didn't want to be mean.

'OK,' I said. 'But you have to promise me that you won't do any more magic or

80

play any more tricks for the rest
of the holiday!'

'I promise!' said Beatrix
eagerly. 'Are you going on the
witch's hat slide? I'll come
too!'

The three of us hurried
up the steps of the witch's
hat. They seemed to go on
for ages and by the time
we got to the top it felt
very, very high. My knees
went a bit wobbly when I
looked down at the tops
of the trees down below,
even though I am used

to flying on a broomstick all the time.

'Let's all go down together!' I
suggested. So Wilbur sat down at the
front, I went behind him and
Beatrix held onto me at the back.
Then we were off!

WHOOOSH!

Round and round and
round the witch's hat we
went, shrieking and
laughing until we landed
in a bubbling cauldron-
shaped pool at the
bottom with a big
SPLASH.

'That was so

much fun!' I gasped. 'Let's do it again!'

The three of us ran back up the twisty stairs, back to the pointy top of the witch's hat.

This time we went down one by one. Wilbur went first and then me.

'Wheeeee!' I yelled as I went round and round and then SPLOSH into the giant cauldron at the bottom. The water seemed more bubbly than before, I noticed. It was starting to slosh round and round like a whirlpool. I managed to swim to the edge of the cauldron and grab onto the side, waiting for Beatrix. The water coming off the bottom of the slide looked fiercer than before too! It was really gushing off the slide, sploshing into the now swirling whirling whirlpool. I frowned. Something didn't feel quite right.

All of a sudden Beatrix came shooting off the end of the slide landing in the centre of the whirlpool. I continued to grip onto the side, watching and waiting for Beatrix to pop her head back up out of the water but I couldn't see her anywhere!

'Beatrix!' I shrieked. Still holding onto the edge of the cauldron with one hand I leaned into the middle of the pool, reaching my other arm to fish her out. I caught Beatrix's arm and dragged her up, coughing and spluttering.

'Quick,' I said. 'Let's get out of here!

Something's gone wrong!'

I dragged Beatrix out of the whirlpool and we both stared at the witch's hat slide, which now looked extremely dangerous with the torrents of water gushing off it.

Beatrix looked a bit shifty.

'You didn't do another spell did you?'
I said.

Beatrix looked down at her feet.

'I just wanted to make it go a bit
faster,' she said. 'Only for my turn! It
wasn't supposed to affect you!'

'Beatrix!' I said. 'You've made it really
dangerous! We have to stop it before any
other witches and wizards come down the
slide!'

'But I didn't bring any potion to undo
it!' said Beatrix looking worried. 'I didn't
think the spell would last this long!'

I stared in panic at the slide. There
were lots of witches and wizards going

up the steps. I noticed that Wilbur was almost at the top again!

'Wait there,' I said to Beatrix. 'If any more witches or wizards come off the end of the slide into the whirlpool then you'll have to reach in and get them out!'

I ran towards Mum and Dad's deckchairs, splashing through the shallow pool water. They were sitting right next to Beatrix's parents.

'Mum!' I said. 'Where's my towel?'

'Under the deckchair,' said Mum, looking up from her Witches Weekly magazine.

I kneeled down and scrabbled underneath the chair, pulling out my towel

and unrolling it. There was my wand! I
had brought it to magic up some snacks
but now I needed it for a more important
reason.

Mum frowned.

'Mirabelle,' she said. 'What in the
name of bats' claws do you need your

wand for?'

'I have to fix something!' I said breathlessly. 'Just trust me! It's an *emergency!*'

Mum narrowed her eyes suspiciously at me.

'How can I trust you after all the trouble you've caused on this holiday already?' she asked. 'Give me the wand please. There's no need for it in the swimming pool!'

'But I *need* it!' I said. 'It's really important!' and then I clutched the wand to my chest and ran off with it.

'MIRABELLE!' shouted Mum,

splashing through the pool after me, followed by Beatrix's mum too.

I was almost at the bottom of the slide when I saw Wilbur whizzing down towards me. He was going so fast he was almost a blur and I could hear him screaming in fright.

I waved my fairy wand, visualising exactly what I wanted to happen.

A shower of stars and sparkles rained down on the slide.

The water slowed, the whirlpool stopped whirling and Wilbur dropped gently into the pool, his head popping back up straight away.

'That slide went *too* fast!' he gasped.

I breathed a sigh of relief just as Mum came up behind me and snatched the wand out of my hands.

'MIRABELLE STARSPELL!' she began.

'Beatrix!' wailed her mum. 'Are you OK? Did *you* go on that slide?'

'I'm fine,' said Beatrix, shuffling her feet nervously on the ground.

Mum glared at me crossly.

'I didn't do anything!' I said. 'I was just *fixing* it!'

Mum didn't look as though she believed me.

Wilbur stared suspiciously at Beatrix and then he did a very un-Wilburish thing.

'Mirabelle *didn't* do anything,' he said.
'It must have been Beatrix! She's the one
who's been causing all the trouble. She put

potions on the dragons during the dragon trekking and turned my spaghetti into worms. Now she's put a spell on the slide!'

Beatrix hung her head looking very embarrassed.

'Is this true, Beatrix?' asked her mum.

'Yes,' said Beatrix in a small voice. 'It *was* all me. And it's thanks to Mirabelle that the slide got fixed! I don't know what would have happened if it hadn't been for her.'

Mum looked surprised but I saw the corner of her mouth twitch into a proud smile. Beatrix's mum on the other hand did not look happy at all.

'Beatrix, what have I told you about

causing mischief?!' she said. Her face had gone all red and she looked like was about to explode!

'I'm sorry!' said Beatrix and then she started to cry. 'I didn't mean to cause so much trouble. I've never had a friend like you before, Mirabelle. I didn't want you to think I was . . . boring.'

'Boring!' I exclaimed. 'I could never find you boring, Beatrix. But I do wish you'd stop getting me into trouble with all your spells! I'm *trying* to be good this holiday.'

'I'm sorry,' sniffed Beatrix again, just as her mum grabbed her hand and began to march her away from the pool.

'I'm going to take away all your potions for the rest of the week,' I heard her say. 'There will be NO more magic this holiday . . .'

Mum, Wilbur, and I were left standing in the shallow water of the pool. Mum looked a little sheepish.

'I'm sorry I didn't listen to you,

Mirabelle,' she said. 'It's just that all those things *did* very much seem like things you would do. And you did sneak your potion kit into your suitcase.'

'It's OK,' I said.

Mum smiled and gave me a big hug.

Chapter SEVEN

Wilbur and I had a great time in the waterpark. We went on all the rides and played in the pool until sunset. Then we went back to the treehouse and had a campfire with Mum and Dad where we roasted marshmallows and sang songs. It was the best day ever!

The following day I bumped into Beatrix at the swamp spa. Her mum was keeping a beady eye on her and she seemed much more subdued.

'I couldn't believe some of the stories you were telling me, Mirabelle,' she said. 'About how you magicked up a dragon and turned your Dad into a frog! I thought you'd think I was so boring!'

'But that's nothing compared to what you told me!' I said in surprise. 'Your stories are even naughtier!'

Beatrix shrugged and she went a bit red.

'I made some of them up,' she whispered. 'I was trying to impress you.'

I stared at Beatrix in disbelief.

'You don't need to impress me, Beatrix!' I said. 'And you definitely don't need to impress me by doing any more magic! In fact, I'd prefer it if you didn't!'

Beatrix beamed with delight.

'Really?' she said.

After that Beatrix and I spent the rest of the holiday together and Beatrix didn't play any more tricks. It was much more fun! Even Wilbur joined in with our games sometimes. By the end of the week I felt really sad to say goodbye.

'I'll miss you, Beatrix!' I said.

'I'll miss you too, Mirabelle,' said Beatrix, shyly handing me a little present. 'I bought this for you at the gift shop. You can open it in the car.'

'Oh, thanks!' I said, feeling touched that she would get me a present. 'Let's be pen pals. We can write letters to each other!'

'OK!' grinned Beatrix happily.

We swapped addresses and then got into our separate cars, waving goodbye to each other. Once we had started driving I opened the little gift that Beatrix had given me. Inside the wrapping was a small wooden box. I flicked open the lid and almost jumped out of my skin.

BOIIIING!

A green witch's head with a long warty nose pinged up at me on a spring.

'Got you!' it cackled.

I squealed and dropped the jack-in-a-box on the floor.

Then I burst into giggles.

Five days was obviously too long for Beatrix to go without playing a trick!

Turn the page
for some
mischievous
things to make
and do!

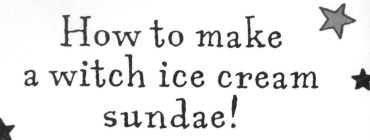

How to make a witch ice cream sundae!

Ingredients

- ★ Your favourite ice cream
- ★ Ice cream cone
- ★ Blueberry ice cream (or any other purple ice cream that you like!)
- ★ Sweets
- ★ Liquorice laces
- ★ Cake decoration edible eyes

Method:

1. Take an ice cream sundae glass, and add a scoop or two of your favourite ice cream to fill up the glass.

2. Add a scoop of blueberry ice cream to the top. This is your witch's head!

3. Make your witch's face with edible eyes, and sweets for the nose and mouth.

4. Add liquorice laces to make your witch's hair.

5. Add the ice cream cone to the top, to make your witch's hat.

6. Enjoy!

Which witchy holiday activity suits you best?

Take the quiz to find out!

1. What is your favourite thing to play on at the playground?

     A. Slide.

     B. Roundabout.

     C. Swing.

2. On a rainy day, what do you most like to do?

A. Get outside and splash in the puddles.

B. Go for a walk, as long as I've got an umbrella!

C. Keep warm and dry inside.

3. What is your favourite animal?

    A. Dolphin.

    B. Dragon.

    C. Owl.

⭐ Results ⭐

Mostly As

You would love the witch's hat slide at the waterpark! Zooming down the slide and splashing in the water would be the best fun ever!

Mostly Bs

Dragon trekking is the activity for you! You'd love to see the great outdoors from the top of a huge dragon!

Mostly Cs

Snuggling up by the campfire at the end of the day would make you happiest. There's nothing better than toasting marshmallows!

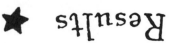

Mirabelle
Gets up to Mischief

From the world of ISADORA MOON

MIRABELLE
Gets up to Mischief

Half witch, half fairy, totally naughty!

Harriet Muncaster

Mirabelle
Breaks the Rules

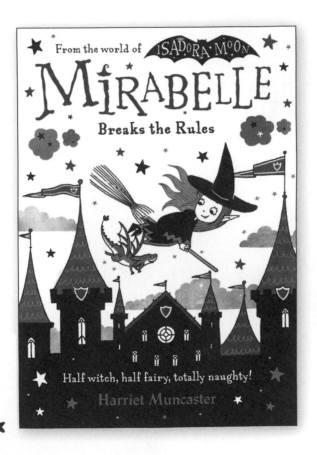

From the world of ISADORA MOON

MIRABELLE
Breaks the Rules

Half witch, half fairy, totally naughty!

Harriet Muncaster

Mirabelle
Has a Bad Day

Read more of
Mirabelle's
exciting antics
with Mirabelle
Breaks the
Rules

Chapter ONE

It was the first day of a new term at witch school and I was up early, before anyone else in my family.

'Let's make breakfast for everyone,' I said to my pet dragon, Violet, as she fluttered in the air next to my ear. 'It will be a nice surprise!' Violet did a little snort and purple flames shot out of her snout.

I hurriedly batted them away with a tea towel. My mum gets funny about scorch marks around the house.

I started to put bowls and plates on the table, and put some bread in the toaster for Mum. We all eat very different breakfasts in my family. My mum is a witch and eats all sorts of horrid things. Her favourite breakfast is spider sprinkled toast. My dad on the other hand, is a fairy. He likes eating flower nectar yoghurt and lots of green salads. Fairies love nature!

The toast popped and I reached for Mum's jar of frizzled spiders.

'Yuck!' I said as I tipped a heap of them

onto her toast.

    Next I put some yoghurt and flower petals into a bowl for Dad and then started to make mine and Wilbur's breakfast. Wilbur is half fairy just like me except he doesn't like to admit it.

He insists that he is a full wizard most of the time. I don't mind my fairy side so much, but I definitely feel more witch! That's why I decided to go to 'Miss Spindlewick's Witch School for Girls'.

As I was buttering Wilbur's toast my eye was drawn back to Mum's spider jar sitting on the counter. A naughty idea floated into my head.

'Go away!' I told it.

But the thought would not go away. My toes started tingling at the idea of mischief.

I pulled Mum's spider jar towards me

and used a fork to scoop out just one little crispy critter. I dropped it onto Wilbur's toast and then quickly slathered it over with jam. He would never know it was there until he felt it crunch in his mouth! I giggled at the thought of him discovering the spider. Both of us hate witch food.

'Breakfast time!' I called up the stairs.

★ ★ ★

'How thoughtful of you to make everyone breakfast Mirabelle,' said Dad as he tucked into his rose petal yoghurt. I smiled sweetly

and watched Wilbur from out of the corner of my eye.

'I hope this is a sign of things to come!' said Mum.

'What do you mean?' I asked.

'Well it's the first day of a new school term,' said Mum. 'I'm hoping you're starting as you mean to go on! I don't want to hear any more reports of mischief from your teacher this year.'

'Oh,' I said and felt my cheeks turn a tiny bit pink. Wilbur took another bite of his jammy toast.

Crunch.

I gulped. Mum

frowned. Wilbur stopped chewing for a moment and then his face turned very white. He spat his mouthful out onto his plate and stared, horrified at the spider legs sticking out of it.

'MIRABELLE!' he shouted angrily. Then he picked up the chewed up mouthful with the spider in it and threw it at me. I ducked just in time!

'Mirabelle!' said Mum and her eyes went very dark and glinty like they do when she's getting angry. But the corner of her mouth twitched slightly. My mum has a mischievous streak inside her too, though she does her best to hide it.

'Sorry,' I whispered, but it was hard to get the word out because I was trying not to laugh. Dad looked genuinely disappointed and was worriedly swirling his spoon about in his yogurt.

'I hope you haven't put any spiders in

MY breakfast!' he said. 'You know I'm a vegetarian! This is really disgraceful behavior Mirabelle. I'm hoping for better from you this year at Witch School.'

By half past eight Wilbur and I were ready by the front door with our broomsticks.

'Have a lovely first day back at school!' said Mum as she kissed us both goodbye.

'And remember to behave yourselves,' said Dad.

'I always behave myself!' said Wilbur indignantly.

'I'm not talking to you,' said Dad and stared pointedly at me.

Harriet Muncaster

Harriet Muncaster, that's me! I'm the
author and illustrator of two young fiction
series, Mirabelle and Isadora Moon.
I love anything teeny tiny, anything
starry, and everything glittery.

Love Mirabelle?
Why not try these too . . .